King Kamaliza

Muli wa Kyendo

Printed and published in the Ushanga Book Series in 2015 by the
Syokimau Cultural Centre, P.O Box 20257– 00100 Nairobi.

Series Editor: Emma Muli

ISBN: 978 9966 7020 2 9

OTHER BOOKS BY MULI WA KYENDO

WHISPERS:
"It's definitely a quick, engaging read with sympathetic protagonist. The story telling is very African in style." — Samir Rawas Sarayji

THE WOMAN OF NZAUI: a play that dramatizes the role of women in African society.

THE SURFACE BENEATH: a novel about the life of Kenyan students in Germany.

Kioko and the Legend of the Plains:
"an incredible story with a tight plot, a character any reader will empathize with, and a wonderful lesson." — Megan Green

CHARACTERS

KING KAMALIZA, a self-styled ruler of Kai, an African country

QUEEN, an ambitious victim of King Kamaliza, otherwise known as Nzuula

KULAYOTE, an ambitious young lawyer

BAKISHA, lawyer and friend of Kulayote

KING KAMALIZA

SCENE ONE

(A large mansion. There is an air of opulence and isolation about the mansion. Action starts with military music. The music has a heavy, defiant beat)

Where are the oppressors
So they may be ashamed?
Yesterday they kept me last on line.
Now, it's about turn,
I am number one.

(Music fades under the sound of the state-of-the-art car of KING KAMALIZA. The car stops outside the mansion.

KAMALIZA is short and hefty with clothes decorated with military medals. He exudes an air of comedy as he marches with pomp and authority.)

(At the door, he knocks confidently.)

Open the door! Open the door! Open the door, my dear!

(Door opens. King Kamaliza enters and pours a drink for himself from a bottle on the table. He gulps it down and belches with satisfaction. He puts down both the glass and the bottle of wine on the large table)

KAMALIZA: *(Turning to Queen, an elegantly dressed woman standing expectant next to him)* The news, my dear, the news! What's new?

QUEEN: Nothing. Nothing is new, my Lord.

KAMALIZA: Nothing is new? What

about my medals? Have you seen me wearing them before?

QUEEN: No. No, I haven't, my Lord.

KAMALIZA: You see, something is new! The medals commemorate a change in me. I am a born again…

QUEEN: … you mean…

KAMALIZA: … no, no!. Not in the Christian sense, though not quite different.

(Pause)

You see, I just rediscovered my heritage as King and ruler of Kai.

(He pauses again. Pours another drink as he paces around the room)

Well, lately I have discovered that there is something special in names…

Something spiritual you could say….

QUEEN: Mmm…

KAMALIZA: ….. something spiritual you could say ….

QUEEN: Mm….

KAMALIZA: *(mimicking)* Mmm… mmm…. What kind of talk is that? You heard me, my dear!

QUEEN: *(Walking over to Kamaliza)* My Lord, what kind of comment do you expect? You even haven't completed stating your thoughts...

(She tries to embrace him)

What has happened to the love that was to be between us? That's what I wonder about my Lord.

KAMALIZA: Love!

(Angrily)

You talk of love when important matters of state lie unattended. And you talk of love!

QUEEN: *(Persisting)* My Lord, they say love is what makes the world go round.

KAMALIZA: You are talking of things I don't understand.

QUEEN: *(Despairing but still persistent)* There are only two things that make the world go round, my Lord.

KAMALIZA: Two things?

QUEEN: Yes, two things…. love and war.

KAMALIZA: Well then, at the moment, we are at war. The state is at war, my dear. Only yesterday, we, my government, that is, executed three senior public servants — ungrateful public servants that I, King Kamaliza, as a benevolent King of this country, had raised from the despicable dust of common humanity. Traitors, they are! Power hungry fools.

Fools who were planning to incite the great people of Kai to rise against me, their beloved King... And the fools were already at work to incite public servants to strike claiming they want more pay... that they want more pay because I, King Kamaliza, raised salaries for myself, my ministers and the army generals.

(Fuming)

Have you heard of such stupidity? Sometimes I wonder where this country would be without me, King Kamaliza!

QUEEN: Mmm....

KAMALIZA: You heard me, my dear! Or are you telling me a story in riddles?

QUEEN: Riddles? No, I am not telling you a story in riddles, my Lord. This is a very plain thing which I have always wanted to tell you. But there hasn't been any opportunity…

KAMALIZA: Obviously there is a story here. There is a very big story. Tell me, my dear, do you know something I don't know?

QUEEN: Yes, I know something which I couldn't tell you unless there was time. And we were in the right place.

(A loud kiss, then in a whisper)

This is the time!

KAMALIZA: *(Relaxing to the new mood)* And the place! This palace, you remember, I built it just for you. Do you remember the millions of shillings I spent on it? And the colourful army parade that opened it?

(Marches as he sings)

Where are the oppressors
So they may be ashamed?
Yesterday, they kept me last on line
Now, it's about turn,
I am number one.

(He laughs noisily)

That's a song I cannot forget. It is as if it was written just for me. As they say, God's about turn…

QUEEN: *(Caught in the enthusiasm)* … has no sound!

(They both laugh warmly)

KAMALIZA: That's quite right. Do you remember the thousands of VIPs —

Very Important People — who attended the opening ceremony of this stately building? The money I spent on this mansion, I always tell you without a boast, is more than a half that which is in the treasury of this country.

QUEEN: I remember many people complained—in the press, in their homes, in the bars…

KAMALIZA: … in fact, e-v-e-r—y where!

QUEEN: But you ignored them all. That's when I realized you are truly the king, the owner of the wealth and land of Kai. You crash all opposition like a bulldozer flattening rocks.

KAMALIZA: *(Flattered)* Who can stand before me? Not even the Americans. And they call themselves the superpower! They threatened to cut their development aid – theirs and that of the World Bank and the IMF and I threatened them back.

(Laughs)

It is not for nothing that I am called King Kamaliza—the King who finishes everything that opposes him. My politics is based on a simple principle: Destroy everything that opposes you!

(He pauses. Then more reflective)

Sometimes I wonder if names truly come from God. Do you think so?

QUEEN: How, my Lord?

KAMALIZA: Just like this — at least this is how I imagine it. That before a soul reincarnates, he appears before the Almighty God. The All Powerful is with his Council of Elders. So these wise Elders ask the poor soul: What do you want to do when you get back on earth?

The poor soul may say: "I want to be a fighter". So the wise souls tell him "Then your name will be such and such and you will reincarnate in Africa where there are plenty of wars for you to fight."

The reincarnating soul can, of course, say, "I want to be a King, a leader of my people". Then the wise souls will tell him, "In that case, here's your name. And here is the place to reincarnate". In my case, the Almighty himself must have said "Your name will be Kamaliza. You will reincarnate in Kai where people need your help. You will never make peace with your enemies. You will crush them instead." At least that must have been so in my case....

QUEEN: Mm?

KAMALIZA: Yes. It must have been so! I must have been born to be a King. Do you know when I was born, a huge cloud of smoke flew out the roof of my mother's house? My mother asked a diviner what it meant — not that she believed him, mark you, not that she believed in diviners — but the diviner told her that the smoke was a sign that a king had been born.

Oh, yes. I was actually born a king! That is what it means.

You see, it was the same with Jesus. The Holy Book tells us that his birth was heralded with many miracles. Even a star was seen ascending in the east... In my case, in the case of King Kamaliza, a cloud of smoke was seen rising up from my mother's house!

QUEEN: Many people praise your confidence.

KAMALIZA: Confidence? No. It is not confidence at all. I just do my work as God ordained me to do. When I overthrew the government of President Polepole, some people condemned me. They said that I was a power hungry army general. But I wasn't. I was just playing my ordained role so that I may rule over my people…..

(He stops abruptly. Then…)

Did I hear gun fire?

QUEEN: Gun fire?

KAMALIZA: *(Ashamed of his fright)* Never mind. In the army, we used to say nobody dies twice. But we were wrong. People die many times over. But that is another story…. As I was saying, my case must have been like that. When Polepole, the soul reincarnate, appeared before the Almighty, he cannot have been convincing, but the Council of Wise Elders allowed him to become president. His fate was that I would overthrow him and establish the dynamic Kingdom of Kai. Don't you think so?

QUEEN: What then do you say of me? What was I born to be? To be used and discarded? Was I born to
become your hideaway mistress?

KAMALIZA: No, my dear. You are not just a mistress. You are the mirror that reflects my true self.

QUEEN: *(Sobs)* Oh miserable fate. Miserable fate that cursed me!

KAMALIZA: Many women in Kai would be glad to be in your position.

QUEEN: In my position? What is my position?

(Sobs)

And to be this when I could be more! When the kingdom could have been all mine!

KAMALIZA: You are an intelligent woman, playing an important role in a great government. You are the proverbial woman that our European friends say is behind every successful man. What more do you want?

QUEEN: Well, my fate must be thus. God created me for it.

(Sobs)

Oh terrible fate that is mine!

KAMALIZA: *(Urgently)* Did you hear gun fire? Did you hear gun fire?

QUEEN: Gun fire?

KAMALIZA: *(Urgently)* Yes. Gun fire, my dear! Did you hear gun fire?

QUEEN: No. I didn't hear gun fire but

I did hear the sound of a car drive past.

KAMALIZA: A car? Drive past? This mansion I built for you, isolated and insulated… who can have the impertinence, the impudence, the insolence, the temerity to drive past here? Who can it be?

QUEEN: Who else can drive past here?

KAMALIZA: You are telling me a story—in riddles. Now you will be plain: Who drives past here, stalking and spying on the King?

QUEEN: Must be your Army General.

KAMALIZA: Who do you mean?

QUEEN: Your Army General.

KAMALIZA: General Akili?

QUEEN: Yes. I mean the same General

Akili.

KAMALIZA : What in God's name would he be doing here? Following me?

Queen: It is a despicable thing, my Lord, especially seeing that you trust him so.

KAMALIZA: There you go again— telling me things in riddles. Be plain, my dear, be plain. Does General Akili come here?

QUEEN: No my Lord, but he has been ogling at me …

KAMALIZA: …ogling at you? That's a very serious crime! Ogling at you? And you gave him no cause?

QUEEN: No cause whatsoever, my Lord. Since you rescued me from the shameful captivity of President Polepole, I have never so much as looked in the direction of another man.

KAMALIZA: *(Relenting)* You remind me of great things, my dear… things that prove to me that you are not just a beautiful face, but that you have a wonderful brain inside your head, too.

(Cunningly)

To me you are worthy more than ten thousand General Akilis put together.

QUEEN : Really?

KAMALIZA: It's a fact. Do you remember the way you helped me get rid of President Polepole?

(Kisses her in mock thankfulness)

Without your help, President Polepole would still be the president of this country. Oh, my dear, you are precious! And you can imagine that President Polepole mistook you for a flower girl in his compound. He didn't know you were the snake in the grass!

QUEEN: *(Offended)* You call me a snake in the grass! For the help I gave you? For making you a king, you call me a snake in the grass?

(Hysterical)

Oh, God of heaven, Oh, Lord Jesus! What role have you ordained for me? To be mocked, hated and abused for my usefulness!

KAMALIZA: *(Actually remorseful)* God forbid that I should sound ungrateful…

QUEEN: Do you trust me?

KAMALIZA: The King trusts no one more than he trusts you.

(Pause)

Did you hear gunfire?

(Sound of moving car is actually heard)

QUEEN: *(Now scared)* No. But I did hear the sound of a moving car! I heard a car drive past!

KAMALIZA: Tell me, who else comes here? Who passes near this palace? Who is stalking and spying on
the King?

QUEEN: I don't know my Lord!

KAMALIZA: Catch him, whoever it is that's trailing the King. Lay a trap and bring him to me. Alive!

(Kamaliza exits, slamming the door behind him. Queen, imitating, sings)

Where are the oppressors
So they may see
In the past they kept me last on line

Now it's about turn
I am number one

BLACK

SCENE TWO

(Scene is the same as before except that Queen is watching herself in a full length mirror, turning this way and that way, obviously happy with what she sees.

Overjoyed, she starts matching and singing again imitating King Kamaliza.)

Where are the oppressors
So they may see
In the past they kept me last on line
Now it's about turn
I am number one

(The singing and matching is interrupted by a knock on the door)

KULAYOTE: *(from without)* Open please! Open quickly!

(Queen opens the door. Enter Kulayote, a youthful lawyer, smartly dressed and full of self-importance)

QUEEN: It's you Mr. Kulayote!

KULAYOTE: Did the King notice anything different?

QUEEN: Notice anything! He heard your car!

KULAYOTE: Heard my car?

QUEEN: Yes, he heard your car.

KULAYOTE: And what did he say? What did you tell him? Did he really know who it was?

QUEEN: Mr Kulayote, if King Kamaliza knew who it was, you wouldn't be talking to me now. You would be dead — dead and ten feet under the soil!

(Pause)

But the king suspects there is someone trailing him, spying on him.

KULAYOTE: Did he seem to suspect anyone in particular?

QUEEN: I wouldn't know. But I know he's working on it. It won't be long before he catches up with you!

KULAYOTE: What did you tell him? Did you work on our plan?

QUEEN: I hinted it might be his Army General.

KULAYOTE: Excellent! Well done! I

sensed he might be around and made a turn to the bush to avoid his guards.

(Pause)
You know the King very well, what do you think he will do with his army general?

QUEEN: The King trusts his army general....

KULAYOTE: *(Sarcastically)* ... and that's not for nothing! General Akili is the last fool in this country. He was born truly to serve... to serve King Kamaliza. If a chance popped up right under his nose for him to be king, he would still serve King Kamaliza.

QUEEN: That's the way of the world. There will always be a king and his servant. King Kamaliza and his Army General Akili

KULAYOTE: That's where you go

wrong — to assume that some people are born servants and others masters. We are all fit to be kings.

QUEEN: You are just trying to be modern and clever. You are trying to impress me with your university school book knowledge. But real life isn't a book. It's made up of hard facts.... Like that King Kamaliza was born to be a king and we were born to serve him.

KULAYOTE: That's absolute nonsense.

QUEEN: That is the absolute truth! Each person is born with his work.

KULAYOTE: Again, that is absolute nonsense.

QUEEN: Well? All monkeys cannot swing on one branch of a tree.

KULAYOTE: But you can get rid of those hanging from the branch and swing on it yourself!

QUEEN: That is what has ruined Kai... that's what has ruined Africa. We all want to be presidents and kings. We don't recognise our different talents... that we can all serve the country and find greatness and satisfaction doing what we are good at. Who will sweep the roads if we are all presidents and kings?

KULAYOTE: The ones who are now presidents and kings! It will be their turn to sweep the roads.

QUEEN: King Kamaliza says that everyone plays his role as ordained by God. A beggar goes to the streets to beg. A priest goes to the pulpit to preach. And a king goes to the palace to rule.

KULAYOTE: Good lessons from King Kamaliza.

(Mocking)

Tell me then, am I fit to be a king?

QUEEN: You! At best you should be an athlete, with your kind of sinewy body. Or you could be a boxer. I think you could better be a thief - crouching in bushes waiting to rob mansions like mine with a name like yours.

KULAYOTE: A name like mine?

QUEEN: Yes, a name like yours! Your name sounds like a hyena's. King Kamaliza says names reveal your destiny.

KULAYOTE: Never mind what you think of me. ….

QUEEN: *(Mocking)* Well, I will tell you, you are fit to be king, Your Majesty! Now tell me, what will I be when you have overthrown the King? Will I be your mistress, hidden in a mansion?

KULAYOTE: No, no, no! You will be a real queen. A real queen living like a real queen.....in a real palace.

QUEEN: What can you give me that King Kamaliza doesn't give me? This mansion, he built for me at a cost of more than a half the money in this country's treasury. The water I drink is imported from the splendid springs of France. The shoes I wear are imported from Italy ....

KULAYOTE: *(Interrupting)* You will be a real queen, just think of that.

QUEEN: You are trying to be smart, but you are not. To tell you the truth, I am tired and sick of being used and discarded.

(Breaks down crying)

Oh, miserable fate that cursed me from my mother's womb! I was only a child, a child in school when it happened...

KULAYOTE: When what happened?

QUEEN: *(Continuing as if she has not heard Kulayote)* When President Polepole kidnapped me.

KULAYOTE: President Polepole? How did it happen?

QUEEN: Heaven forbid that I should remember those things! We had gone to entertain him at the State House—small children from our school—when his wicked eyes fell on me. Oh, may God erase that day from memory!

It was at night, I remember, when his guards came to take me away. My father said no — he wanted me to finish school. The guards coaxed and threatened. My father knew he could never win. I remember my father's sad face—his helplessness as he watched me being bundled in President Polepole's huge Mercedes. I cried for my father's sake — no, for my sake. I was another victim of president Polepole's wickedness.

KULAYOTE: *(Embracing her)* Do not cry. President Polepole placed you in a better position to help this country... To change it for the benefit of us all!

QUEEN: *(Facing Kulayote with a surprised look. Then she resumes her story)* I vowed to revenge. I vowed to avenge my father and my honour.

(Pause)

My father died shortly afterward because of shock — or despair — I don't know. What I know is that I swore to avenge him.

That's why I helped King Kamaliza to overthrow President Polepole. I wanted revenge. I wanted freedom. And King Kamaliza promised all these. But now look at what I have got! I exchanged a tyrant for a monster!

(She buries her face in her palms, crying).

KULAYOTE: Take this handkerchief and dry your tears. If beauty were something that could be measured, yours would outweigh that of all the women of Kai put together.

(A thunderous knock on the door is heard. Enter BAKISHA, young man, smart but looking frightened)

BAKISHA: Christ Jesus! Kulayote, you are resting as if you were in your house! We have limited time!

(To Queen)

Have you been able to create suspicion between the King and his Army General?

KULAYOTE: Bakisha, the lady has already given indications to the King—reasons to doubt the general.

BAKISHA: Kulayote, let the lady speak for herself.

(To Queen)

Have you?

QUEEN: The King trusts his Army General

BAKISHA: Did you hear that Kulayote? The King trusts his Army General.

(To Queen)

As you know, creating doubts and conflict between the King and his Army

General is an important part of our government takeover plan. The King and the General united, we cannot defeat them. But if they are fighting, we will walk past them and into the State House.

QUEEN: Mr Bakisha, the King trusts his army general!

BAKISHA: Kulayote, I told you this lady was not the right person to entrust with our plan. Now we are as good as dead

(To the Queen)

Now lady, does the King know anything about our plan?

QUEEN: Not from me.

BAKISHA: Ah! So he knows!

QUEEN: I wouldn't know but he heard

your car.

BAKISHA: Jesus Christ on earth! He heard our car! Then we are dead. Now I will never see my son Joseph again…. and my wife, Jane!

(Breaks down crying)

And to know I could have avoided this!

(To Kulayote)

Kulayote, you put me into this. I told you I didn't want to get involved…

KULAYOTE: No use regretting now, Bakisha. We are together in this.

BAKISHA: *(Hysterical)* Take this gun and shoot me, quick! Shoot me until I am dead. A quick death is better than being detained in Kamaliza's torture chambers.

QUEEN: What? What did you say just now?

BAKISHA: King Kamaliza heard our car! The next thing we know, we are being pulled by horses along the streets, handcuffs and all on our arms and feet. Then we are being taken to dark rooms with ice cold water and crawling bugs And we are being interrogated and beaten by gum-munching policemen of King Kamaliza. We are being beaten and tortured senseless. No. No. Better a quick death with a gun!

KULAYOTE: Not so fast, Bakisha. An honourable death is in the battlefield.

BAKISHA: *(Very frightened)* I heard a car. I heard the engine noise of a car! It must be the King. Kulayote, I am running away. It's better to die running.

(Flees, running very fast)

KULAYOTE *(To Queen)* Keep your word! You know what it means to all of us!

(Exit Kulayote)

(We hear military song)

Where are the oppressors
So they may be ashamed?
Yesterday they kept me last on line.
Now, it's about turn,
I am number one.

(Music rises to a crescendo and then fades as King Kamaliza enters with matching but calculated, steps)

KAMALIZA: Any progress my dear? I smell the aroma of strangers around here. Have you trapped the fools?

QUEEN: My Lord, only the King enters this palace.

KAMALIZA: Very well.

(Silence as Kamaliza moves about the room as if to inspect it)

Today the King of Kai has performed some important functions. He has ordered the execution of three other senior government officers involved in a plot to take power from him.

And the King has also issued a warrant of arrest for two youthful lawyers named Kulayote and Bakisha...

QUEEN: *(Shocked)* What!?

KAMALIZA: You happen to know them?

QUEEN: *(Composing herself)* Who? Me? Know them? How could I know them?

KAMALIZA: Sorry, my dear, but I happen to know that the foolish boys have infiltrated all important places.

QUEEN: This lonely mansion, my Lord, would you call it an important place?

KAMALIZA: Yes. The answer is, yes and no.

QUEEN: My Lord, I would do nothing to harm the King….

KAMALIZA: No, you wouldn't. I am just taking a little precaution — following my instinct, you would say. My instinct tells me the young men will surface here.

QUEEN: No need to worry my Lord. I would turn them over to you the moment they enter the mansion…

KAMALIZA: Good, my dear. Do let me know if you spot them!

(Exit Kamaliza, slamming the door behind him)

BLACK

SCENE THREE

(Scene is as before. QUEEN is matching up and down the room as she sings, imitating King Kamaliza).

QUEEN: *(Sings as she marches)*

Where are the oppressors
So they can be ashamed?
Yesterday they kept me number last,
Today, it's about turn
I am number one

(The music and the singing are stopped

abruptly as a knock is heard on the door.)

(Enter Kulayote and Bakisha)

QUEEN: What! You two again! Now you have walked yourselves into King Kamaliza's trap. He was here just now, looking for you two …!

KULAYOTE: Never mind. You are talking to the man who is going to be king any moment now!

BAKISHA: Yes, you are talking to the new king.

QUEEN: Oh, I see! You already have a king and his servant! King Kulayote and his servant Bakisha! Have you two gone crazy! Don't you know the risk you are taking? How can you take power from King Kamaliza with your bare hands?

BAKISHA: We count on the dissatisfaction of the populace. The university teachers are on strike over pay… the doctors are going on strike tomorrow… and all the civil servants will go on strike the day after. Everyone will soon be on strike except King Kamaliza and his Army General who are fleecing the country dry! Since King Kamaliza took over power, none of us Kai people is happy. The country has become poorer and poorer by the day as King Kamaliza plunders the economy. We have found out King Kamaliza's weakness. We have found out his secret weapon.

We are going to turn it against him. And you will see us take over power with everyone applauding.

KULAYOTE: If names have meaning as Kamaliza says, then his is to finish the country's wealth.

BAKISHA: See how he has ruthlessly killed everyone who dares criticise him?

See how he has filled every public office with relatives and tribesmen. See how he has given his relatives and tribesmen every government contract… we cannot say we are people living in a free, prosperous country. Can we? Can we!?

KULAYOTE: Now, you are seeing the future leaders of Kai. We are the leaders. The Americans have agreed to back us up. And the British too, have agreed. In fact, they all have agreed to help the economy back on its feet as soon as we have taken over power.

BAKISHA: And that may as well be tonight….

(A knock on the door is heard. King Kamaliza calls from outside)

KAMALIZA: Open the door! Open the door!

QUEEN: See what trouble you have

brought me! Run, hide under the bed. I'll try to get him out quickly.

(Aside)

Get courage, my dear
The moment I have dreaded has now come
This is the moment!
What words can describe
The fear within my heart?
Here I stand condemned — or nearly so
— To certain death. And never again
Shall I nurse my sacred ambition
To be real Queen. A Queen of Kai.
Instead I will take one last look
At the beauty of this stately house
That King Kamaliza, in his wanton wickedness
Built just for me! Just for me!
Then I will go to meet my worst.

(Loudly)

Coming, my Lord!

(Door opens. Enter King Kamaliza. First there is confidence in his footsteps. Then suddenly he falters)

KAMALIZA: *(Alarmed)* What! A frog! A frog in this mansion! Who brought a frog into the mansion?

(He chases after it, trying to shoot the frog with a gun but it flees into the bedroom. King Kamaliza hesitates at the door)

(Aside)

There the frog goes, just as it was prophesied
That doom is spelt if ever a frog enters the mansion,
And yet this prophesy - can it really be true?
Can it be from the self-same source
As that which prophesied me King?
It would be folly to believe otherwise
With this natural confluence—it would

be difficult.
I must resign myself to this two-faced
thing
That prophesied me King.
From now, everything will go into
Eternal silence. All that I have achieved
In the past, will get buried deeply
Into the nothing of the present
To confirm the folly of faith
Build on a string of air.

(To Queen)

I ask you for the last time: Who brought
the frog into the mansion?

(Grabs her neck as if to strangle her)

Who brought the frog into the house?

(Reappearance of the frog catches his attention)

There flees the frog yet again!

(He pursues it into the bedroom where Kulayote

and Bakisha are hiding. His gun is poised to shoot)

BAKISHA: Okay, now the game is over! We are as good as dead!

KULAYOTE: Not so fast, Bakisha!

KAMALIZA: *(Standing face to face with Kulayote and Bakisha)*

Ah! It's you two! This is the thanks I get for helping you make money with government contracts. I gave you the chance to make wealth. And this is what I get in return… Yes, you are dead! You are dead and finished with. If you have prayers to say, say them NOW!

(Kamaliza closes his eyes tight, his gun trained on Bakisha who is shaking with fear)

BAKISHA: I told you, Kulayote, this would not come to any good.

(Hysterical)

Now all I have worked for is gone. Everything is gone!

(He shoots at King Kamaliza and kills him)

We are as good as dead Kulayote! We are dead!

(He shoots and kills Kulayote. Then he flees at great speed past Queen and out the door. We can hear his words, "Better to die fleeing than to face King Kamaliza's firing squad" as they recede into the distance.)

(There is deafening silence. Then we hear the military song)

Where are the oppressors
So they may be ashamed?
Yesterday they kept me last on line.
Now, it's about turn,
I am number one.
(It starts at a low note rising to a boom before

dying out as we return to Queen who stands alone in a room in the mansion, telephone in her hand)

QUEEN: They are all dead. They killed themselves pursuing power which I now hold in these hands of mine. It's mine for the taking. Here I am now, alone and free. I can draw my line anyway, anywhere, anyhow I want. It will still be a straight line. And most of all I can be a real Queen …. if I choose. And if I have the confidence. As Kulayote says, I can be a real Queen, the ruler of Kai even if my name Nzuula, does not mean much… In fact my mother said it means a loafer, an idler, a degenerate, one who wanders about purposelessly like the water beetle. But not now when I hold power in my hands... Mine to take if only I have the confidence. And what will I tell the people?

(She presses numbers on the phone , then speaks)

The King is dead! …. General Akili, the King is dead! Come quickly. The king is dead… killed opponents and self….

(Up military song to the end)

Where are the oppressors
So they may be ashamed?
Yesterday they kept me last on line.
Now, it's about turn,
I am number one.

KING KAMALIZA

OUR MISSION

The mission of the Syokimau Cultural Centre is to develop and spread, through literature and art, value systems that foster cultural understanding across ethnic and racial groups.

Our vision is of communities where people live in harmony, enjoying and appreciating their "otherness" and the beauty of their cultural diversity.

Printed in the United States
By Bookmasters